BILL GILLHAM was formerly director of the MSc course
in Educational Psychology at the University of Strathclyde
and is a well-known educational psychologist, academic and researcher.
He is the author of around 60 children's books. His first book
for Frances Lincoln was **First Words: Babies Start Here!**
Bill lives in Glasgow, Scotland.

CHRISTYAN FOX has written and illustrated lots of books for children,
many with his wife, Diane. He is the illustrator of the very successful
Piggy Wiggy series. This is his first book for Frances Lincoln.
Christyan lives in Surrey, England.

For Charlie, who is
learning to count.
Bill Gillham

And for Harvey,
who might learn
to count one day.
Christyan Fox

First published in Great Britain in 2005 by
Frances Lincoln Children's Books, 4 Torriano Mews,
Torriano Avenue, London NW5 2RZ

www.franceslincoln.com

Distributed in the USA by Publishers Group West

First paperback edition 2006

British Library Cataloguing in Publication Data
available on request.

ISBN 10: 1-84507-564-1 3737 4641 4/08
ISBN 13: 978-1-84507-564-4

Illustrated with Adobe Photoshop

Printed in China

9 8 7 6 5 4 3 2 1

How many
SHARKS
in the bath?

Bill Gillham
Illustrated by Christyan Fox

FRANCES LINCOLN CHILDREN'S BOOKS

How this book works:

- Read the questions

- Count the animals

- Point to the numbers

The youngest children may only be able to count from 1 to 3 but there's at least one of these numbers on each page. You help with the bigger numbers.

0 none
1 one
2 two
3 three
4 four
5 five
6 six
7 seven
8 eight
9 nine
10 ten

0 none
1 one
2 two
3 three
4 four
5 five
6 six
7 seven
8 eight
9 nine
10 ten

0 none
1 one
2 two
3 three
4 four
5 five
6 six
7 seven
8 eight
9 nine
10 ten

0 none
1 one
2 two
3 three
4 four
5 five
6 six
7 seven
8 eight
9 nine
10 ten

0 none
1 one
2 two
3 three
4 four
5 five
6 six
7 seven
8 eight
9 nine
10 ten

0 none
1 one
2 two
3 three
4 four
5 five
6 six
7 seven
8 eight
9 nine
10 ten

0 none

1 one

2 two

3 three

4 four

5 five

6 six

7 seven

8 eight

9 nine

10 ten

0 none
1 one
2 two
3 three
4 four
5 five
6 six
7 seven
8 eight
9 nine
10 ten

0 none

1 one

2 two

3 three

4 four

5 five

6 six

7 seven

8 eight

9 nine

10 ten